In memory of Lilian Carter   D.S.
To Daisy Carter, now a butterfly   C.B.

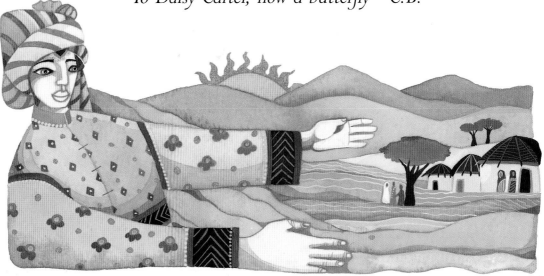

The Lion Book of
WISDOM STORIES
from around the world

Retold by DAVID SELF
Illustrated by CHRISTINA BALIT

LION
CHILDREN'S

Contents

Tell Me a Story

We all enjoy stories. We like listening to stories and we like telling stories.

We like stories that make us laugh. Sometimes we enjoy a scary story!

We tell stories about things we have done and seen and heard — so we can share them with our friends. Telling a story helps us to remember what happened.

Some people have made up stories so that the people who hear them will remember other important things — things such as how good it is to share what we have, to help one another and not to waste time arguing. Sometimes, these stories are about people. Other times, they seem to be about animals but are really about people as well!

Each story in this book was first told in a different country — to teach the people there who heard it a wise truth.

I hope you enjoy these 'wisdom stories' from around the world — and I hope they make you a little bit wiser!

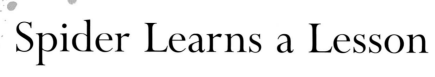

Spider Learns a Lesson
or How Wisdom Spread Around the World

Long, long ago, there lived a spider named Kwaku Anansi. He was very good at tricking people. He knew that. But he also knew that there were lots of things he didn't know. For one thing, he didn't know what made you really wise, someone other people would respect.

'Yes, that's it,' he said to himself. 'I want to be wiser than anyone else. I'll find all the wisdom in the world – and keep it for myself!'

Besides being a trickster, Anansi was very selfish.

Having decided what he wanted to do, Anansi set about hollowing out a calabash. A calabash is a kind of gourd and Anansi wanted to use it like a bowl to hold all the wisdom he could find. When he'd hollowed it out, he went from home to home asking everyone to give him their wisdom.

Before long, his calabash was overflowing with wisdom.

'I must now be the wisest person in the world,' he said to himself. 'I must find a good hiding place for the wisdom so I don't lose it and so no one else can find it.'

At that moment, he saw a very tall tree. 'That's a good place,' he said to himself. There were spiky branches sticking out of its trunk which would make it difficult for any other creature to climb it. 'Only a spider could climb to the top of such a tree. If I hide all this wisdom up there, nobody will ever steal it from me.'

But the tree trunk was so steep it was hard to climb, even for a spider. Anansi would need all his eight legs to cling onto it – and he wouldn't have any spare legs to carry the heavy calabash with all the wisdom in it.

He had an idea.

He found a long strip of cloth
and tied one end around his waist.
Then he used the rest of the cloth
to tie the heavy calabash to the front
of his tummy. He was ready to start
climbing the tree.

But as soon as he started, the
calabash got in his way. He couldn't
reach round it to grip the tree with
his legs. He tried and he tried – and
got very hot and very angry.

Before long, Anansi's young son
Ntikuma came by. 'What are you
doing, Dad?' asked the young spider.
This made Anansi even crosser because
he didn't like his son seeing him fail.

'Can't you see?' asked Anansi.
'I'm trying to get this calabash full
of wisdom to the top of the tree.'

Ntikuma watched him for a
moment. 'It's getting in your way,
isn't it?'

'I know that!' shouted Anansi,
angrily.

'Why not tie it to your back?
Then it won't get in your way and
your legs could grip the tree.'

Anansi thought about this. 'You just
scuttle off home!' he told Ntikuma.

He was even more angry now because he didn't want to admit his son had been speaking good sense.

Ntikuma knew when it was wise to get out of his father's way so he scuttled off home.

Anansi undid the calabash and then tied it behind his back. He found he could now climb the tree without too much difficulty. And that's what he did. When he was near the top, he stopped for a rest. Even though he'd nearly done what he wanted to do, he still wasn't happy.

He'd realized that even his young son was wiser than he was. 'I've been everywhere. I've collected all the wisdom I can find and still there are other people wiser than me,' he thought. 'So what's the point keeping all this wisdom to myself? Sharing wisdom is the way to be truly wise.'

So Anansi untied the calabash and swung it around in the air. All the wisdom fell out and spread all over the world.

'Now anyone who wants to be wise will have to listen to people from all around the world,' he said.

The Lost Coin

There was once a woman who had ten silver coins. Because they were made of real silver, each one was very valuable.

One day, she lost one of the coins. She was sure it was somewhere in her house. Because she lived in a hot country, her house had few windows, which stopped the sun from making it hot indoors. That meant it was dark inside so she lit a lamp. It was still quite dark and she couldn't see the coin.

So she started to brush the floor.

Suddenly she heard a little clinking sound and knew she'd found the coin. She bent down, felt around – and there it was!

She was so happy that she called all her friends and neighbours and said, 'I'm so happy I've found the coin I lost. Let's have a party.'

And that's what they did – because it's always right to celebrate when something that's been lost is found again or when anything that's gone wrong is put right.

The Eagle and the Jackdaw

At the top of the mountain perched a huge eagle. Halfway down the mountain, there grew a tree. In the tree sat a jackdaw.

In the valley below, where the grass was green, a shepherd guarded his sheep.

The eagle had wings that stretched wide whenever he opened them, a strong beak that could grip like metal and talons as sharp as the claws of a tiger.

The jackdaw was a very handsome bird with his sleek black feathers. As he sat in his tree, he thought how handsome and how clever he was. 'I'm one of the best,' he sang out loud.

At that moment, the eagle noticed that, far below, a young lamb had strayed away from the rest of the flock of sheep and their shepherd.

With wings outstretched, the eagle swooped down to the valley. He seized the lamb in his talons and flew back to the top of the mountain to enjoy his meal.

'That's a very easy way to feed yourself,' thought the jackdaw. 'Why shouldn't I do that?'

So he too swooped down from his tree to the valley below. But the jackdaw wasn't as clever as all that. He tried to seize an old ram, a big heavy sheep with long fleecy wool.

The ram was too heavy for the jackdaw to lift and the jackdaw's claws became tangled in the long straggly wool. He found he couldn't escape and began to squawk.

The shepherd saw what was happening and quickly came over. He seized the jackdaw and untangled his claws from the wool — but he wasn't going to let the jackdaw go free!

'Thought you'd have one of my sheep, eh?' he said. 'I'm taking you home to be a pet for my boy.' Which is what he did.

'Thank you, Dad,' said the boy. 'What kind of bird is this?'

'It's a jackdaw, son,' said the shepherd. 'Only a jackdaw. He thought he was as clever and as strong as an eagle.'

'He was too proud!' said the boy.

'And you know what they say?' asked his father. 'Pride goes before a fall.'

How to Be Happy

She wasn't a very nice woman. She wasn't a very kind person. She never thought about the needs of other people. She was really rather grumpy – and she never felt happy.

But then, one day, she went out in the midday sun. It was a time of day when most people stayed in the cool of their homes. And, as was usual at that time of day in that country, it was very hot indeed.

On the pavement, she saw a dog. It was lying down, stretched out – and too tired to find any shade. Indeed, it was too weak even to pant. The woman realized it was dying of thirst.

In that country, people didn't like dogs. Dogs sniffed nasty, unclean things. Dogs were dirty. Dogs were to be avoided. But, surprisingly, this woman suddenly felt sorry for the dog. 'It needs a drink,' she said to herself. Further along the road, she knew there was a well. Deep down the well was fresh water. So the woman hurried to the well – but the bucket and the rope people used to draw water up out

14

of the well were missing. 'What shall I do?' she thought.

Suddenly she had an idea. She took off one of her shoes and tied it to the black scarf she wore around her neck. Slowly and carefully she lowered the shoe down the well until it dipped into the water and filled up. Even more carefully, she pulled it up. Some of the water spilled out and the shoe leaked a bit.

'Better than nothing,' she said. And she carried the shoe back to the dog, hobbling a bit because she had one shoe on and one shoe off.

By now the dog was nearly dead. She knelt down and gently poured some water over the dog's lips. Soon the dog began to drink from the shoe and before long it was strong enough to give her foot a grateful lick.

Soon the dog was well enough to stand up and walk.

And as the dog walked away, the woman felt strange. She'd never felt like this before. Then she realized, 'I'm happy! I'm happy!' And she put her shoe back on and went on her way, smiling and singing, 'I'm happy!'

Later that day, she thought about what had happened. 'That must be the way you become happy,' she said to herself. 'You do it by making others happy!'

Happy Ever After
Under the Banyan Tree

Once there was a banyan tree. It's a kind of fig tree. It grew in the land we call Bhutan, near the great Himalayan mountains; a tiny country squeezed between the much bigger countries of India and Tibet.

Near the banyan tree lived four creatures: an elephant, a rabbit, a monkey and a partridge. It was a lovely place to live but the four of them weren't happy. They kept having quarrels.

Usually, they quarrelled about the banyan tree. Each of them thought it belonged to him. The elephant was sure it belonged to him. 'This is my tree because I saw it first. I've always rested in the shade.'

That made the monkey laugh. 'Listen to me, Elephant,' he said. 'Do you see any fruits on this tree?'

The elephant looked at the tree. 'Well, no. But what's that got to do with it?'

'Simple,' said the monkey. 'It hasn't got any fruit because I've been eating its fruit for ever and ever. Long before you first saw the tree, and long before you first came to rest under the tree, I was feeding on the banyan fruit. That means the tree is mine!'

Then the rabbit spoke up.

'You're both wrong. I came along and licked the dew on the banyan leaves and then nibbled its leaves when it was just a tiny plant, growing close to the ground. That was long before the monkey ate its fruit and long, long before the elephant saw the tree and came to rest under its branches. So that means it must be my tree.'

The partridge, who was a very wise old bird, had been listening carefully to them all arguing away. Finally he spoke.

'You're all wrong. Even longer ago, I pecked up a banyan seed and brought it here in my mouth. I spat out the seed, scratched the ground and then covered the seed up with soil. And it was that seed which grew into the plant that the rabbit nibbled, and later grew into a tree which bore fruit that the monkey ate – long, long before the elephant ever saw the tree and came to rest under its branches. So that means the tree must be mine.'

'Oh,' said the rabbit.

'I never knew that,' said the monkey.

The elephant just nodded.

There was a silence – then the elephant, the monkey and the rabbit all spoke at once. 'The partridge must be telling the truth. He must have been the first to know the tree.'

There was another, longer silence.

'So if that is the case,' said the elephant, 'we shall have to ask the partridge if he minds sharing his tree with us.' And before they could say anything else, the partridge spoke up.

'Of course you can share my tree,' he said. 'So long as I can rest in its branches.'

'And you're happy if I nibble the leaves I can reach where its branches grow down to the ground?' asked the rabbit.

'And is everyone happy if I eat its fruits when they grow again?' said the monkey.

Suddenly they realized they'd all be happy if they shared the tree. 'In that case,' said the elephant, 'there's not much point quarrelling.'

So the four creatures became friends again and happily shared the tree together. The partridge hid in its leaves, the rabbit nibbled the lowest branches, the monkey ate its fruit – and the elephant not only rested in its shade but used his trunk to reach the highest leaves for them all to enjoy.

The other animals in Bhutan saw them living peacefully together – and sharing the banyan tree. From then, the elephant, the monkey, the rabbit and the partridge were always known as 'the four good friends'.

A Bowl of Milk

They had no home. They were shepherds and they moved from place to place with their families – and their flocks of sheep. When the sheep had eaten all the grass in one place, they moved on in search of new pastures where their sheep could graze on fresh grass. People who live like this are called nomads.

These nomads wandered around central Asia, searching for good grazing land. After many, many years, they found a place where there was always good pasture. They decided to settle there. It was in that part of India called Gujarat, near a place called Sanjan.

After they had lived there for some time, they began to feel it was home. They were no longer nomads.

Years went by. This was now their country. They had their own ways of doing things. And they had their own leader: a wise and good prince called Jadi Rana.

Around this time, far away, another group of people were forced to leave their homeland. That was called Persia but we now know it as Iran. These Persians who had to leave their homeland became known as Parsis.

After a very long journey across deserts that were scorching hot during the daytime and bitterly cold at night, they came to the sea. There, they got on ships and sailed to India. They landed near to Sanjan.

The leader of the Parsis sent a message to Prince Jadi Rana. 'We had to leave our homeland and we have suffered many hardships on a long journey in search of a new home. Please will you let us settle in your country?'

Jadi Rana did not want more people in his country. He was not being cruel but he was afraid there wouldn't be enough room for more people to make their home there. But he didn't want to be rude – and he didn't speak the language of the Parsis.

He thought for a while and then he sent a bowl full of milk, filled to the brim, to the Parsis. This was to be a sign that the land around Sanjan was full: there was no room for the Parsis.

The leader of the Parsis was just as wise as Jadi Rana. He understood what the prince meant by sending him the bowl full of milk. And he knew exactly what to do.

In front of the prince's messenger, he took some sugar and put it in the milk. The sugar dissolved at once. The milk didn't overflow. None was spilt. Instead, the milk became sweet-tasting.

He sent the sweetened bowl of milk back to Prince Jadi Rana. The prince saw at once what the leader of the Parsis was saying. Just as the sugar had mixed easily with milk without overflowing, so his people would mix with the people of Sanjan. They would all fit into the one country – and make that country a sweeter place. There was nothing to fear.

Just to be safe, Prince Jadi Rana said that the Parsis must learn to speak his people's language, Hindi, and to live as they did. If they agreed all of this, then they could live in his country and they would fit in as well as the sugar had mixed with the milk.

The Parsis promised this and so they were allowed to enter the country and settle there.

Since then, the Parsis have learned to speak Hindi and have lived in India as Indians – and have done much good for the country. Prince Jadi Rana's people learned that there is no need to fear foreigners: two peoples can indeed live happily together.

Don't Argue!

Three men were on a long journey, in a very hot country. By late afternoon, they were very hungry and very thirsty.

Suddenly, they spotted a coin lying on the road. But no sooner had they seen it than they started arguing how to spend it.

The first man said they should spend it on something tasty to eat.

The second man said they should spend it on something filling to eat.

The third man disagreed with both of them. 'No, no. We must spend it on something to quench our thirst.'

They argued for a long time, getting more and more hungry and thirsty until another man came along. 'What are you arguing about?' he asked. They told him how they each wanted to use the coin.

'Let's walk on to the next village,' he said.

There, he took the coin and went to buy them a big bunch of grapes, which he divided between them.

'At last! This is something tasty to eat,' said the first man, happily enjoying the sweet taste of the grapes.

'This is something really filling to eat,' agreed the second as he munched on the grapes.

'This is something to quench my thirst,' said the third as the juice filled his mouth.

'So why did you waste time arguing?' asked the stranger.

The Ant and the Grain of Wheat

It had been a good year. First came the rain to water the ground. The wheat seeds put up shoots. Then came the sun and the shoots grew. In the long hot days of summer, the wheat ripened. Then the men came and harvested the wheat.

They didn't gather every grain. Some grains fell to the ground and there they stayed – until an ant found one of them.

'Food!' he said to himself.

Even though the grain was nearly the same size and the same weight as him, he wriggled it onto his back. Then he started to plod slowly back to his anthill, where he lived with hundreds of other ants.

Even though it was a very heavy load for an ant, he didn't give up. He knew the ants would need all the food they could find for the winter months ahead.

As he came to the edge of the wheat field, the grain of wheat suddenly spoke. 'Why don't you leave me here?' it asked.

The ant stopped.

'If I leave you here,' he puffed, 'we shan't have enough to eat in the winter.'

'But this field is my home,' said the grain of wheat. 'I belong here.'

'You are made to be eaten,' said the ant.

'I'm not just food,' replied the grain of wheat. 'I'm a seed as well.'

The ant had never heard about seeds.

'If you leave me here,' said the grain of wheat, 'the wind will blow soil over me. The rain will water me. The sun will make me grow – and I shall become a stalk of wheat.'

The ant thought about this.

'You mean, if we don't eat you this winter, there will be more of you next year?'

'Exactly. You can have one grain now or have a much greater harvest in the future.'

'Are you sure?'

'It's the miracle of life. Dig a little hole, put me in it – and come back next year.'

The ant decided it was better to be patient than greedy.

The following year, the ant returned. The grain of wheat, like many other seeds, had grown into a stalk. And, of course, there was a whole field of wheat, waving in the breeze.

A Loving Gift

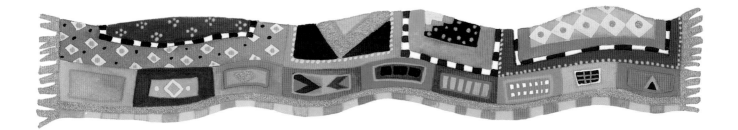

Daud was a weaver. He lived in a village in India and wove beautiful carpets. He used the very best threads of red, dark blue and gold to make elaborate patterns in his carpets. Each one took a long, long time to weave.

Because of this, his carpets were very expensive. Even so, every time he finished one, rich people came to see him – each wanting to buy his newest carpet.

One day, Daud decided he didn't want to sell his next carpet. It would be a gift: a present for someone special. This person was a very wise teacher and in that part of India, the word for 'teacher' is 'guru' – which is why he was known as 'the Guru'. And because Daud had heard him teaching and found that what he said was very helpful, he wanted to give him a present.

Daud set about weaving as good a carpet as he knew how.

It took him a long time. After many days' careful work, it was finished. 'It's good,' he said to himself. Many people came to him, admiring the carpet and asking to buy it. 'Thank you, but no,' said Daud. 'This carpet is going to be a gift.'

One rich man insisted, 'I'll give you twice as much as anyone else for your carpet.'

'That is generous,' said Daud, 'but this carpet is not for sale.'

He took it to the Guru.

'Will you please do me the honour of accepting this gift?' he asked. 'And use it whenever you wish to sit down.'

He said this because, in India at this time, people did not use chairs but spread a covering on the floor and then sat, cross-legged, on the covering.

'That is very kind. Thank you,' said the Guru.

Daud smiled. He was glad the Guru had accepted his present.

'But you see,' went on the Guru, 'the grass is the only carpet I need. It's good enough for me.'

Daud looked disappointed.

'Yet I should like to accept your gift if it may be put to better use,' said the Guru.

'How?' asked Daud.

'You see that dog over there with her puppies? She's weak and can't keep them warm. In fact, they are dying from cold. Please spread your carpet over them and fetch them some milk and food.'

Daud thought for a moment. It was a very good carpet to give to a dog. But then he saw the look on the Guru's face and knew that this was important. He spread the carpet on the ground, gently moved the mother onto part of it and then placed her puppies by her. He folded the rest of the carpet over them to protect them from the cold. Then he went to get them food and drink.

The Guru was now really pleased and Daud knew they had both done a good thing. He felt good. So did the dog and her pups, who grew strong and well – thanks to the loving gift of the carpet.

Silver on the Hearth

The farmer worked hard but the soil on his land was poor. Crops didn't grow well, so he and his wife were often short of food and, because they had nothing to take to market to sell, they were often short of money.

One day, he was weeding his field. Near its edge, a prickly bramble stem caught his coat and tore it. 'This mustn't happen again,' he said to himself.

So he dug around its roots and pulled the bramble out of the ground. Underneath it was a large jar made of straw. He dug it out of the ground and removed its lid. The jar was full of silver coins.

At first he was really excited. Then he thought, 'It's not really mine. Someone must have put it here for safety. I'd better leave it hidden.'

At the end of the day, the farmer left the silver where he'd found it and went home. He told his wife what had happened. She was furious! 'You stupid man! Why did you leave it at the edge of our field? That silver would have made us rich!'

It was no good his saying he'd done the right thing. She carried on shouting – so loudly that their neighbour heard all she said.

That night, the neighbour crept out of his house and went to find the silver. Because the moon was shining, he soon found the spot where the farmer had been digging – and quickly found the jar.

He took it home, happy to have cheated his neighbour. He opened the jar. A poisonous snake popped its head out. The farmer quickly pushed the lid back on the jar.

'That farmer and his wife were playing a trick on me, trying to kill me!'

He went outside, got a ladder and put it against the farmer's house. Then he took the jar, climbed up onto the roof – and emptied the jar down the chimney.

Next morning, the farmer went downstairs into his kitchen. There, on the hearth where the fire usually burned, was one dead snake and a pile of silver coins.

When his wife came into the kitchen, the farmer smiled happily at her. 'We're no longer poor!'

His wife gave him a hug. 'You were right after all. You did the right thing, and your honesty has been rewarded,' she said. 'No one could say you don't deserve it now.'

Not Just a Pawn

Two boys decided to play chess. One of them took the box of chessmen out of his toy cupboard. They started to arrange the chessmen on the board for the start of the game.

But there was one important piece missing. One of the knights was no longer in the box.

Then they noticed that there was an extra, unimportant little pawn left in the box. They decided to put a chalk mark on it to mark it out from the other pawns and then use it as the missing knight.

When one of the boys moved this pawn two squares forward and one square to the side (just as a knight moves in a game of chess), a real knight said to it, 'You're not a proper knight. You're only a pawn. You should move just one square at a time.'

But the boys knew what the knight had said. 'He may look like a pawn,' said one of them to the knight, 'but he's doing the work of a knight.'

'Yes,' said the other boy. 'You should judge a person by what he does, not by what he looks like.'

33

Trust the Donkey

She was very important. She was the daughter of the chief of a group of Native Americans who lived on the Great Plains. That meant she was very, very important indeed.

When she grew up she married and, in time, became the mother of twin sons. She was very happy.

As the babies grew older, their grandmother made two saddle bags for them and gave them one of her donkeys. 'When you travel,' said the old lady, 'my two grandchildren will be comfortable and safe. This donkey will carry your babies safely in these saddle bags, on either side of his back. You will always be able to trust the donkey.'

One day, the chief's daughter and her husband were ready to journey to a new camping place. Her husband brought out his finest pony and put the saddle bags on its back. 'There,' he said, 'my sons shall ride on a proper pony. That donkey is fit to carry only our pots and kettles.'

So his wife loaded the donkey with their belongings and then laid their skin tent and the tent poles across the donkey's back.

No sooner had she done this than the donkey began to bray and fight and kick. He made a huge noise, broke the tent poles and tore the tent. Pots and kettles went flying everywhere.

They could do nothing with him so they went to ask the babies' grandmother how to make the donkey behave. She roared with laughter.

'I said the donkey was for the children,' she cried. 'He's insulted by being made to carry pots and kettles!'

She put the saddle bags over the donkey's back, fetched the children and

put them in the bags. At once, the donkey quietened down.

   The man and his wife and several others from the camp set off, all on horseback – followed by the donkey, carrying the babies.

   After several hours, they passed through a valley overgrown with bushes. There, a group of their enemies sprang out, making terrifying whooping noises.

A great battle began. At last the enemy was defeated and rode away. The man turned to his wife and smiled in triumph. 'You've kept my two sons safe, I hope?'

She looked around. Where were the babies? The donkey was missing! The babies were missing! 'Oh no,' she said, bursting into tears. 'They've gone! I was so afraid for you. I was watching the fight and I never saw they'd gone,' she said.

They searched and searched. For a long time they searched – but in vain. In the end, they gave up and slowly and sadly rode back the way they'd come. The man said nothing and his wife was still crying.

Just as it was getting dark, they reached the camp. There, beside the grandmother's tepee, stood the donkey with the two babies gurgling happily in the saddle bags.

The grandma and the donkey seemed to be smiling at one another. After a moment, the old lady turned to the man and his wife. 'You forgot what I said.'

'What was that?' asked the man.

'I told you that you'll always be able to trust the donkey.'

Axe Porridge

The soldier was walking home from fighting in a war. He was cold, tired and hungry – and very glad to reach a village just as it was getting dark.

He knocked at the door of the first cottage he came to.

'Please, have you any food for a hungry soldier?' he asked the woman who opened the door.

The woman had plenty of food but she was very mean – so she pretended to be very poor.

'I'm just a poor old woman,' she said. 'You can come in and rest for a while but I've nothing to give you to eat. I've not even had anything myself today.'

'Never mind,' said the soldier and sat down. Then he noticed the axe the woman used for chopping firewood. 'If you've really nothing to eat, we could make some axe porridge.'

'Axe porridge? What's that?'

'Lend me your axe and a pot of water,' said the soldier.

The soldier washed the axe, filled the pot with water and put it on the fire. Then he put the axe in the water and waited till it began to boil. The woman watched, full of curiosity.

'Shame you've no salt,' said the soldier. 'It would taste better with salt.'

'I've got salt,' said the woman.

He stirred the salt into the water.

'It's a pity you've no oats,' he said.

'I've got oats,' said the old woman and fetched a sack of oats.

The soldier stirred in the oats. 'Of course, a bit of butter would help.'

'I've got butter,' she said. He stirred that in as well – and soon the mixture was a thick, creamy porridge.

'It's ready to eat,' said the soldier. 'We just need to get rid of the axe.' And he took it out of the pot.

They sat down and shared the porridge. 'It tastes good,' said the woman. 'I'm really enjoying this. I'm so glad you came and showed me how to make axe porridge.'

The soldier didn't say anything.

Why the Wasp Can't Make Honey

Long ago, all the animals had to go to school. The birds lined up for singing classes and nest-building lessons. The cows had to learn how to chew grass so it would turn into milk. The hens had to learn how to lay eggs without breaking them. Lizards learned their trick of changing colour, and glow-worms had to learn how to glow at night.

Each of the other insects had to go to school as well — and some of them were cleverer than others. That didn't mean the clever ones did well at school.

The wasp was very clever but also rather naughty. He never stayed where he was meant to be. He was always buzzing about, disturbing and upsetting the other insects who were trying to learn. No wonder he didn't do very well in lessons.

The bee was quite different. He wasn't quite as clever as the wasp but he worked slowly and carefully, concentrating on what he was meant to be doing.

The teacher in the animal school was a wise old mongoose. She was very strict – but then she had to be, teaching so many different things to so many different animals. And the bee and the wasp were both meant to go to her class to learn two quite difficult things: hive-building and honey-making.

The wasp liked hive-building and could soon build a hive very much more quickly than anybody else. He became very boastful and, as soon as he had built a hive, he started interrupting everyone else in class.

The mongoose was angry. 'If you don't behave, I'll send you out of the class,' she said. The wasp quietened down – for a while.

Soon, the class was ready to move on to honey-making.

The mongoose told them that the first thing they had to do was collect the nectar they would need to make honey. She told them which were the best flowers to visit to find the best nectar.

'I'm not doing that!' said the wasp. 'I'm not going to stick my nose in flowers and get covered in messy, sticky pollen! I'm far too clever and far too handsome to do that!'

But the bee buzzed off slowly, carefully sniffing all the flowers until he

found the ones he'd been told to look for. Then he pushed inside the flower and collected the sticky pollen.

'You do look a mess!' buzzed the wasp as the bee flew slowly back to school.

When they had all returned, the mongoose asked them how much nectar they had each collected. The bee had gathered more than anyone so the mongoose was very pleased. 'Well done, well done,' she said. 'And now what about you?' she said to the wasp.

Of course the wasp had nothing to show the

teacher. 'If you can't be bothered to do what you're told,' said the mongoose, 'there's no point you coming to school. Off you go. You're not staying in my class.'

And that's what happened. The wasp never came back to school and never learned how to make honey. The bee finished all his lessons in honey-making – and set himself up in business. His children and his grandchildren and all his relatives learned how to make honey, and bees have gone on making honey ever since.

Which just shows that anyone can do well by listening to a wise teacher.

As for wasps, they just buzz about angrily – because they're cross they never paid attention at school. In fact, they're still so cross that they sting anyone who gets in their way.

The Most Precious Gift

A long time ago, a great sailing ship was getting ready to leave port for a distant country. Going on board were many wealthy merchants. All the valuable things they hoped to sell in that country were being loaded into the ship's hold, down below deck. There were clothes made of the finest silk. There were jewels, gold and silver and many, many cases of expensive wine.

Among the passengers on the ship was a stranger; a man the other merchants did not know.

'What do you trade in?' they asked. 'What do you bring to sell?'

'The most precious gift in the world.'

'What's that?' they asked. But he'd say nothing more.

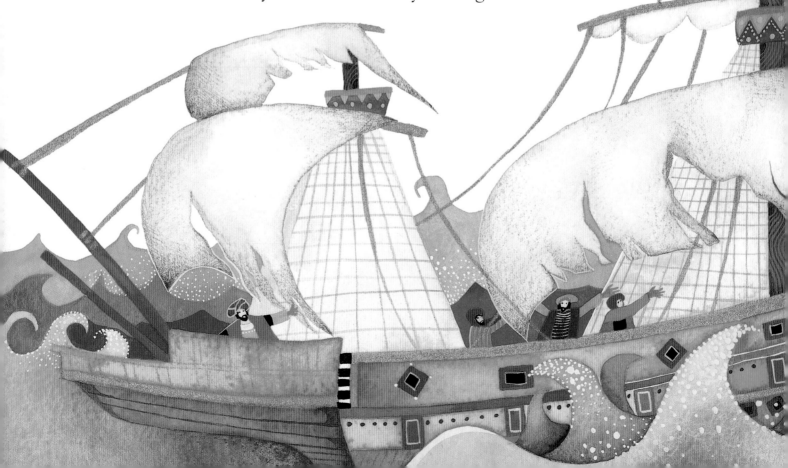

Secretly, they went below deck to see if they could discover what he'd brought on board. They checked every packing case but all they could find were their own cases. When they realized the stranger had no baggage at all, they began to laugh among themselves. 'He's not a proper merchant. He's brought nothing to sell!'

Soon the ship set sail. After several days, a great storm arose and the ship was badly damaged. The sails were torn to ribbons, the mast was broken and soon the ship was drifting helplessly towards some jagged rocks.

With a great crash, the wind drove the ship onto the rocks. It stuck fast. The passengers and crew were able to scramble ashore but the wind and waves attacked what remained of the ship. Soon it split apart and all the cargo was washed out to sea. All the merchants' gold and silver and jewels (and the wine) were lost.

When the merchants went ashore, they found they had reached the country to which they had been sailing. They made their way on foot to the city where they had hoped to sell their goods. Instead of arriving with plenty of things to sell, they came empty-handed. Instead of being wealthy, they had to beg for food and somewhere to sleep.

Like them, the stranger had nothing. But, instead of begging, he went to a public meeting place and spoke to all the people there. What he said proved he was a very wise and learned man. Indeed, it turned out that he had spent his whole life studying the books of the law.

The people of the city were so pleased to meet such a wise person, they asked him to stay with them as their guest. They also paid him to teach in a local college called an academy. Many people came to listen to him as he explained the law and why people should keep it.

After several weeks, it was time for him to return home. The people were sad to see him go but they gave him many presents.

The merchants (who had spent all the time begging in order to stay alive) heard all this and they were astonished that such a man could be so popular. They went to him privately and asked if he could help them to return to their home country.

'We've begged enough to live on – but we've no spare money to pay for our journey home,' they explained.

The man told the people of the city what the merchants needed. The people said they would pay for the merchants to travel on the same ship as the teacher – only because such a wise man had asked on their behalf.

So the merchants and the teacher went on board the same ship together. As they put out to sea, the teacher said to the merchants, 'You laughed at me. You thought I brought nothing with me to sell. But I brought something really valuable: the gift of wisdom. It is more precious than any jewels or silver or gold.'